Meg Mackintosh

and

The Mystery at Camp Creepy

A Solve-It-Yourself Mystery

by Lucinda Landon

Secret Passage Press

North Scituate   Rhode Island

Books by Lucinda Landon
Meg Mackintosh and the Case of the Missing Babe Ruth Baseball
Meg Mackintosh and the Case of the Curious Whale Watch
Meg Mackintosh and the Mystery at the Medieval Castle
Meg Mackintosh and the Mystery at Camp Creepy
Meg Mackintosh and the Mystery in the Locked Library

About the author
Lucinda Landon has been an avid mystery fan since her childhood.
She lives in Rhode Island with her husband, two sons, two dogs,
one cat and one horse. Their old house has a secret passage.

Copyright © 1990 by Lucinda Landon

First Secret Passage Press Edition

Library of Congress Cataloging-in-Publication Data

Landon, Lucinda.
  Meg Mackintosh and the mystery at Camp Creepy : a solve-it-yourself mystery / by Lucinda Landon.
  p. cm.
  Summary: While attending summer camp for the first time, Meg tries to solve the mystery of the camp's legendary ghost. The reader is challenged to interpret each clue before Meg finds the solution. (1. Camps — Fiction. 2. Ghosts — Fiction. 3. Mystery and detective stories. 4. Literary recreations)
I. Title.
PZ7.L231735Men 1990   (Fic) — dc20   88-38466
ISBN 1-888695-03-X
(previously published by Little, Brown and Company ISBN 0-316-51367-9) AC

10   9   8   7   6   5   4   3   2
BP
PRINTED IN THE UNITED STATES OF AMERICA

For the cousins:
Trevor, Hilary, Noah,
Micah, Eliza, Lizabeth,
Zoë, Alexander, Eric,
Brian, Gayle, Jessica,
Reed, Emily, and Alice

The creepiest story of all," began one of the camp counselors, "is about the ghost right here at Camp Crescent."

Meg Mackintosh edged closer to the campfire to hear.

"A long time ago, this land belonged to an old man named Stuart," the counselor continued. "He lived in the old shack where we keep the canoes. Ever since he died, they say you can hear his ghost rustling around in there at night."

"And on a misty night," continued another counselor, "you can see Stuart's ghost paddling his canoe across Crescent Lake."

Just then everyone heard noises in the distance.

"What was that?" they all asked the counselors.

The sounds seemed to be coming from the old canoe shack. A shiver went up Meg's spine. The counselors exchanged glances, their eyebrows raised. "Even they're getting spooked," Meg thought.

"Everybody's here at the campfire. Who could that be?" she overheard her cabin counselor, Annie, whisper to another counselor.

"That's enough ghost stories," Tim, the camp director, announced abruptly. "Time for bed."

All the campers hurried back to their cabins. Meg was staying in the Chipmunk Cabin with seven other girls. As they got ready for bed, she heard a lot of whispering, much more than there'd been the first two nights at camp. One girl began crying a little. Meg doubted anybody was going to sleep very well that night. Just before Annie turned out the light, Meg reached under her cot, grabbed her detective knapsack, and took out her flashlight, pencil, and a postcard.

She snuggled into her sleeping bag and wrote:

July 3

Dear Mom and Dad,
  Camp is pretty good - so far.
This is only the 3rd night —
27 to go. Tonight one of
the counselors said there's
a ghost here. I'm not scared
but you do have to go out to
another building to go to the
bathroom. I just hope I
don't have to go in the middle
of the night. Pet skip for me.
I miss you,
Love, Meg

P.S. Please send some
Size D Batteries for
my flashlight. xo.

Meg Mackintosh
Chipmunks
Camp Crescent
Belden, Maine
04856

Mr + Mrs. J. Mackintosh
P.O. Box 222
Foster, Rhode Island
02825

POST CARD

When she was finished, she tucked the postcard
under her pillow and fell asleep.

Meg woke up early the next morning. She quickly dressed, then tiptoed out of the cabin. "I'm glad I brought my detective kit to camp," she said to herself, as she flung her knapsack over her shoulder and darted down the path toward the lake.

Soon she came upon a very old, small house — Stuart's shack. "Looks pretty spooky, even in daylight," Meg thought, as she cautiously peered through the broken windows. It was dark and very quiet inside. She thought she heard something rustling around, but decided it was probably just her imagination.

Meg looked carefully around the outside of the old shack. Under the dried leaves, she found two old rusty cans, some broken glass, an old piece of wood with nails in it, and a brown and white feather. "But no footprints," she muttered to herself.

She snapped a photo with her instant camera.

Then she bent down to pick up the feather. "Hmm, I wonder what kind of bird this is from?" She studied it carefully. Just then the morning bugle rang out. She shoved the feather in her pocket and ran back toward the lodge.

Meg caught up with two other campers on their way to breakfast. They had stopped at the Camp Crescent sign and were studying it intently.

"I think I heard the ghost again last night, only near the kitchen," confessed a girl from the Otter Cabin.

"Maybe it was a raccoon trying to get into the garbage," suggested a boy in a baseball cap.

"Which one's the haunted shack?" asked the girl.

"It's here." Meg pointed.

"I bet it's creepy," said the boy. "Hey, we should call this place 'Camp Creepy' instead of Camp Crescent!" he exclaimed.

They all laughed at the new name and headed to breakfast. But on the way, Meg thought more about the clues around Stuart's shack. "There has to be a logical reason for those noises," she told herself.

Meals were served in the lodge, where everyone sat at long tables. After breakfast, Tim announced all the activities campers could choose from for the day: swimming, sailing, tennis, canoeing, hiking, nature lab, archery, softball, and arts and crafts.

Not one camper signed up for canoeing that day. Most campers wanted to go sailing or try archery. But Meg had her mind set on one activity in particular.

IF YOU WERE MEG, WHAT WOULD YOU SIGN UP FOR?

At the nature lab, Meg examined her feather with her magnifying glass. "I'm trying to figure out what kind of bird this feather came from," she told a boy named Hank. They looked in some bird books, but so many of the feathers were brown and white that it was impossible to tell anything from just one small feather.

Later that morning, after the Chipmunk Cabin campers went swimming, Meg went to the trading post to buy stamps. She quickly wrote a postcard to her grandfather and mailed it with the one to her parents just as the noon bugle called everyone to Assembly Field.

July 4

Dear Gramps,
Camp is okay. A kid plays the bugle all the time like Dad did when he went to camp. We had pancakes for breakfast this morning but not as good as yours. I've been swimming a lot and they say there's a ghost here! I'm trying to figure out what's going on. See you in August. Miss you lots,
Love, Meg-O

Meg Mackintosh
Chipmunks
Camp Crescent
Belden, Maine
04856

Mr. George Mackintosh
Hillside Lane
Rockdale,
Massachusetts
01931

POST CARD

The older kids, from the Bobcat Cabin, had made up new verses to the Camp Crescent song and were chanting them loudly.

> In a shack on Crescent Lake —
> Camp Creepy, Camp Creepy,
> There's a ghost that makes you shake —
> Camp Creepy, Camp Creepy.

He rows his canoe on a misty night —
Camp Creepy, Camp Creepy,
If you meet Stuart you'll die of fright!
Camp Creepy, Camp Creepy!

"Happy Fourth of July, everybody!" Tim interrupted their singing to make an announcement. "To celebrate we're going to have a special cookout down at the campfire for lunch. Let's go!"

Each camper found a long stick with a pointed end and stuck a hot dog on it. Then they cooked their hot dogs over the campfire. For dessert they toasted marshmallows.

After lunch, Tim whistled to get their attention. "Now for a special treat! We're going to have a treasure hunt. One of our counselors, Kip, planned the whole thing, and only he knows where the answer is. He has a few days off, but he left me this envelope with the first clue."

"Clue?" thought Meg excitedly, almost dropping her marshmallow.

"This really looks like quite a mystery," Tim continued, "so listen carefully. The clues lead to a special prize that must be found by sundown tonight! All the clues must be solved to find the prize, so there are no short cuts. Now which one of you wants to read the first clue?"

"I do!" Every hand shot up right away.

Tim held the envelope above them.

In the excitement, everyone grabbed at the envelope and somehow Meg's fingers reached it first. But before she realized what was happening, it slipped from her fingers and landed right in the fire.

"Oh no!" she cried.

Tim quickly grabbed a hot-dog stick and tried to rescue the clue. But by the time he speared it out of the flames, it was just a charred scrap of paper.

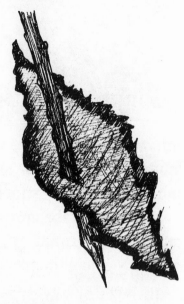

"Look what you've done!" one of the older boys yelled at Meg. "The clue is burned!"

All the other campers looked at Meg as if they blamed her, too.

"I'm sorry," she said, looking down at her sneakers. "Rats," she thought to herself. "I bet nobody will talk to me for the rest of July."

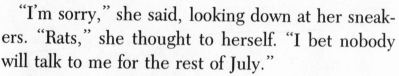

There was a brief silence.

Then Tim patted Meg on the back. "I've got a good idea!" he said cheerfully. "We'll climb Magic Mountain. It's a great hike for the Fourth of July. We'll have another treasure hunt when Kip gets back."

As they all headed back to their cabins to get ready for the hike, Meg stopped her counselor. "Annie, I don't feel very good. Hot dogs sometimes give me a stomachache." But she knew it wasn't from the hot dogs.

"Maybe you'd better go to the infirmary," suggested Annie. "You can stay there with the nurse until you feel better."

As Meg walked slowly toward the infirmary, she stopped by the campfire. The stick Tim had used to stab the burning clue was still there. Meg pulled what was left of the clue off the tip and studied it. There was a tiny bit of writing left on it. "Maybe I can figure this out," she thought. "At least it's easier to decipher than a ghost's footprint!"

WHAT DO YOU THINK IT SAYS?

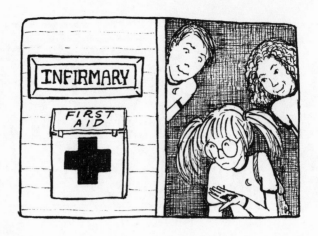

"Catch something?" Meg was still wondering when she reached the infirmary steps.

"Are you sick?" came a voice from inside.

Meg looked up to see two faces gazing at her from the doorway.

"The nurse will be right back," the boy told her. "I'm Russell."

"I'm Meg. Uhh, I have a stomachache."

"Hey, you're the one who ruined the treasure hunt." Russell scratched his arms. "I was at the campfire just before my counselor sent me here. I have a rash."

"I'm Tina," said the girl.

"You're a Chipmunk, too, aren't you?" Meg asked her. "Where have you been lately?"

"I've been sort of sick," she said shyly, "homesick, that is. And last night that ghost story gave me nightmares."

"Maybe she's the one who was crying at night," thought Meg. "I know how you feel," she admitted. "I was a little scared about that, too."

"Is that what's left of the clue?" asked Russell, looking at the scrap in Meg's hand.

"Yes. I think I might be able to figure it out." She looked at them hopefully. "Maybe you two could help me?"

"Maybe." Russell thought for a second. "I do like puzzles. And so far, this camp hasn't been much fun. Okay, I'll help."

"How about you, Tina?" Meg asked. "If we all put our heads together, I bet we could solve it."

"Okay." Tina looked at the clue. "It looks like something about a cat, but I haven't seen any cats around here."

"No, it says 'catch,'" Russell pointed out. "Let's see, maybe a catcher's mitt or catch a fish."

"But this looks like an animal's footprint here, don't you think?" asked Meg. "Part of it's missing."

"I bet it's a cat's print!" cried Tina.

Meg thought for a minute. "I know how to figure it out! Follow me."

"The nurse will be looking for us," warned Tina.

"She said she'd be back in twenty minutes," said Russell. "That gives us ten. Let's go."

WHERE DID MEG TAKE THEM?

Meg led them to the nature hut. "Look at the chart on that wall." She got out her magnifying glass. "Let's compare prints."

They studied the poster and clue for a few minutes. "I think it looks like a fox print," said Meg.

"Catch a fox? That's impossible," Russell objected.

"It does look like a fox print," said Tina. "But why is 'cat' underlined?" She glanced at her watch. "We'd really better get going," she added nervously.

Meg, Tina, and Russell hurried back to the infirmary. They were just catching their breath when the nurse walked in.

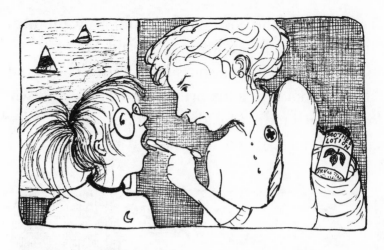

"Hello, I'm Ms. Kane," the nurse introduced herself to Meg. "What seems to be the problem?"

Meg told her about her upset stomach, even though it didn't really hurt anymore.

"You all look a bit flushed. I hope there's nothing going around." Ms. Kane examined their throats and took their temperatures. "Russell, here's some lotion for your arms and legs. It looks to me like you've got poison ivy. Now don't scratch! That'll just make it worse. I have to go to the office for a while, but I want the three of you to stay right here and rest."

"It's going to be hard solving a mystery with her around!" Russell whispered after she left.

Meg and Tina nodded in agreement. Then Meg carefully took the burned clue out of her knapsack.

"What do you think this 'X' means?"

"X marks the spot," said Russell, scratching his ankles.

"Something about an X where you can catch a fox?" suggested Tina.

Meg scribbled in her notebook, Tina twisted her hair, and Russell scratched. They were all puzzled.

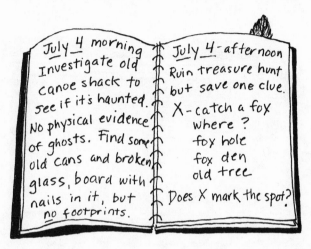

July 4 morning
Investigate old canoe shack to see if it's haunted.
No physical evidence of ghosts. Find some old cans and broken glass, board with nails in it, but no footprints.

July 4 - afternoon
Ruin treasure hunt but save one clue.
X - catch a fox
where ?
fox hole
fox den
old tree
Does X mark the spot?

"I've got an idea," Meg said suddenly. "We've got to go look."

"Where?" asked Russell.

Meg just said mysteriously, "Come with me and find out."

"I'll stay and watch for the nurse," Tina offered. "If she gets back before you do, I'll think of something to tell her."

Meg nodded, then she and Russell slipped out of the infirmary and headed to the other side of Camp Crescent.

WHERE DID THEY GO?

"Hey, this is my cabin," said Russell.

"It's the 'X' on the clue that made me wonder," explained Meg. "There's an 'X' in the word *fox*, and there's a sign that says foxes on this cabin. Maybe X *does* mark the spot."

Russell rolled a log beneath the sign to stand on. He stepped up and slid his fingers behind the sign.

"I think we've got something here!" he shouted, taking a small piece of paper from behind the "X." He jumped to the ground and quickly opened the note.

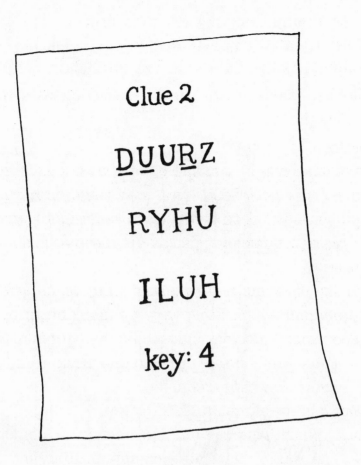

Clue 2

DUURZ

RYHU

ILUH

key: 4

"It looks like a secret code!" exclaimed Meg. She got out her notebook and pencil, sat on the ground, and started writing.

"Just like in spy stories." Russell sat down next to her. "I've read a zillion of them. It looks like an alphabet code. There's even a key. There's a hint to unraveling the code."

WHAT DO YOU THINK "KEY: 4" MEANS?

Meg wrote out the whole alphabet. "The key is four. I bet that means that the key alphabet starts with the fourth letter — D." She wrote a second alphabet underneath the first, starting with the D under the A.

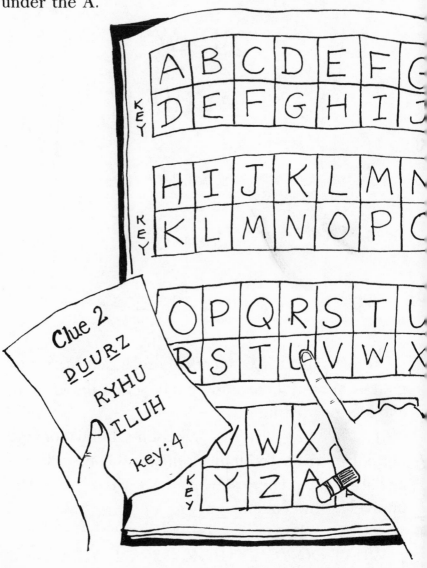

In a few minutes Meg and Russell had deciphered the clue.

WHAT DO YOU THINK IT SAYS?

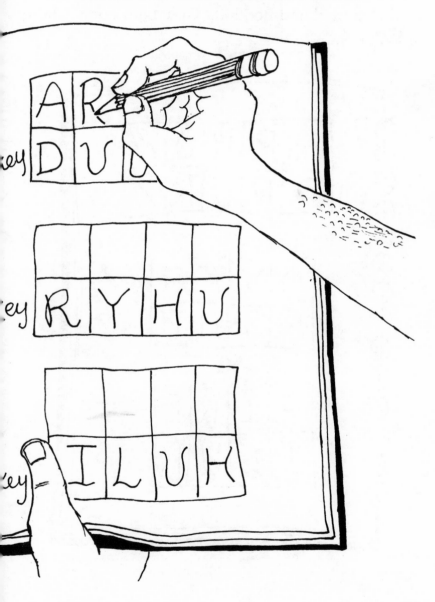

" 'ARROW OVER FIRE,' " Russell read. "What does that mean?"

"Hmmm. Something to do with the campfire?"

"Or . . ." Russell made a gesture.

Meg smiled and nodded. They both knew where to look first.

"We don't have much time." Meg said.

"I know a shortcut," Russell said. "I went this way yesterday."

They followed a dark path through the woods.

WHERE DID THEY GO?

"There's the archery range," said Russell, "and this is where I stopped to read a book so nobody would bother me." He pointed to an old tree stump.

Meg and Russell searched the entire range and checked all the arrows. "I really think we're on the wrong track," Meg said finally. "Let's look somewhere else."

Just then they saw Tina racing toward them.

"Lucky I found you," she said, catching her breath. "I told the nurse that you went to the lodge to get a book, and she sent me out to bring you back!"

"Great thinking, Tina," said Russell.

"And perfect timing," Meg added mysteriously. "I have an idea. Let's go."

WHAT DOES MEG WANT TO SHOW THEM?

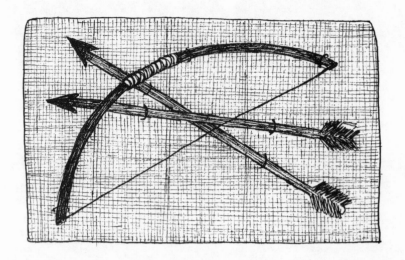

Once they were in the lodge, Meg pointed to the far wall. "Look at the *arrows* displayed *over* the *fireplace.*"

"Incredible!" Russell stared at the arrows.

While he quickly explained Clue 2 and the deciphered code to Tina, Meg got a chair and dragged it in front of the fireplace. Standing on it, she examined the arrows. "Could you please hand me the tweezers in my detective kit?" she asked.

"Wow, you really are serious about this detective stuff!" Russell handed her the tweezers. "You even have a fingerprinting kit in here!"

Meg carefully removed a small piece of paper that was tucked in between the feathers at the end of one arrow. "Look, another clue!"

"Now we're really getting somewhere," said Tina excitedly. "Let's see!"

```
Clue 3

Beware of me
And my leaves of 3
The answer to clue 3
Is safely set
3 away and under 3
```

"Three leaves? Under three? This is confusing," Russell sighed.

"I saw something with three leaves on it," Tina muttered.

"We'd better get back," warned Russell, heading for the door.

"Aren't we forgetting something?" asked Meg.

"What?"

"Our alibi. The books for us to read!"

They quickly took some books from the shelves in the corner of the lodge and hurried out the door.

WHERE DID TINA SEE THE "LEAVES OF THREE"?

As Meg, Russell, and Tina slipped back into the infirmary, the nurse glanced up from her phone conversation, giving them a stern look. They quickly lay down on their cots and pretended to read.

"Look!" Tina whispered, a few minutes later. She pointed to the bottle the nurse had given Russell. "Three leaves!"

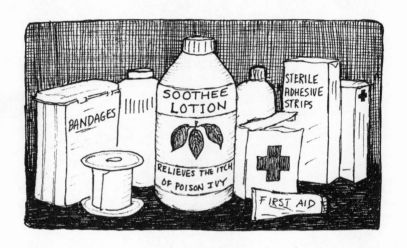

"Uh, ohh," said Russell. "Those leaves *do* look familiar. And I think I know where I ran into them — if only we could sneak back out."

"Tina and I could distract the nurse," suggested Meg. "Listen . . ." She whispered her plan to Russell and Tina. Then Meg and Tina crept into the bathroom.

"Ms. Kane!" called Tina. "We need you! Meg's stomach is upset again."

The nurse rushed into the bathroom.

Russell quickly stuffed the pillows under the blanket on his cot and propped the book on the side. Then he quietly went out the door.

"Could I please have some ginger ale?" Meg begged the nurse. "My mother always gives me some, to help settle my stomach."

"Okay, dear, I'll go over to the kitchen and get some." Ms. Kane tiptoed past the cots. "That's nice; Russell is taking a little nap."

WHERE DO YOU THINK
RUSSELL REALLY IS?

"How could I have been so stupid! Some shortcut!"
Russell scolded himself. "I sat right in the middle of
it! I hate you, poison ivy!" He scratched his arms

and legs furiously. "Now what did that clue say again?" He pulled it out of his pocket and read:

Clue 3

Beware of me
And my leaves of 3
The answer to clue 3
Is safely set
3 away and under 3

WHERE IS THE ANSWER TO CLUE 3 HIDDEN?

"That must mean three feet away from the poison ivy," Russell thought. Then he imagined a circle around the tree stump and about three feet from it. Just outside the circle, he spotted a rock cairn — a pile of three rocks that hikers use to mark a trail. He excitedly lifted up the rocks. Underneath was a small folded piece of paper. Another clue!

He grabbed the note and, not taking time to read it, raced back to his infirmary cot — minutes before the nurse returned.

Only after Ms. Kane brought Meg the ginger ale and was back at her desk and out of earshot did Russell quietly unfold the clue and show it to the other two.

Clue 4

A flying fish
Goes up with the sun
Find me when
I'm down again

" 'Flying fish.' What do you think that means?" Tina looked at Meg.
"I'm not really sure."
All three of them were puzzled.

WHAT COULD CLUE 4 MEAN?

"Maybe we should wait until the others get back from the hike and show them the clue," suggested Russell.

"But the mystery has to be solved before dark," Meg reminded him. "They may not be back in time. And the prize might be ruined if it's found after dark." She paused for a minute. "I think this clue has something to do with the sun going up and down. Or is it the fish going up and down?"

"It doesn't make sense," protested Russell. "I haven't seen any flying fish on the lake. And how could there be a clue on a fish?"

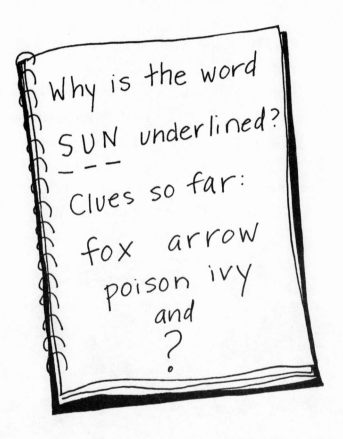

Why is the word SUN underlined?

Clues so far:

fox arrow poison ivy and ?

Meg jotted in her notebook and they studied the clue for what seemed like a long time. They wanted to go down to the lake to look around, but couldn't think of any other excuses to get out of the infirmary. Ms. Kane hadn't budged from her seat except to look in on them every once in a while.

Suddenly they heard the voices of the returning campers.

"Wow!" exclaimed Meg, glancing at her watch. "It's almost six o'clock. And we still haven't figured this out!"

Just then Ms. Kane walked in. Meg quickly covered her notes.

"Meg, how's your stomach? I want to check your throat, Tina. And, Russell, that lotion seems to be helping your poison ivy." Ms. Kane looked them over carefully. "I think you're all well enough to join the others now."

Do-do-dodedo-do-do-dodedo! rang out.

"There's the bugle call for the lowering of the flag," Ms. Kane told them. "You'd better hurry."

"Oh, I almost forgot," said Tina. "I'm signed up to do tonight's flag ceremony."

Suddenly Meg's eyes brightened. Before Tina could dash out, Meg quickly whispered in her ear.

"What's going on?" Russell asked Meg a few minutes later, as they headed toward Assembly Field.

Meg told him what she had told Tina.

"The clue *has* to be there!" he shouted excitedly.

WHAT DID MEG TELL TINA AND RUSSELL?

While the campers gathered in a circle around Assembly Field, four campers stood in formation in the middle to perform the flag-lowering ceremony. Tina would pull the ropes, one camper would keep the flags from touching the ground, and then the other two would carefully fold them. There were always two flags to bring down: first the American flag and then the Camp Crescent flag.

"I knew I'd seen a fish flying somewhere," Meg whispered to Russell, as they gazed up at the Camp Crescent flag.

"A flying fish that goes up and down with the sun," added Russell with a grin.

As Tina pulled the Camp Crescent flag down, she spotted what Meg had told her to look for — a small piece of paper attached to one of the clips that held the flag. Before anyone noticed, she quickly slipped it off and shoved it into her back pocket. When both flags were folded, the four campers solemnly carried them back into the lodge, with the rest of the campers following to find their seats for dinner.

Meg, Russell, and Tina ended up at separate dining tables, so they had to wait all through dinner, announcements, and songs to find out what the latest clue said.

They finally met again out on the lodge porch. Tina pulled the clue out of her pocket and opened it.

They all read in silence.

Last Clue

Take clues of flora,

Fauna, fin & feather—

Find the prize

When put together

_ _ _ _ _ _ _   _ _ _ _ _

"What does it mean?" Tina wondered. "This is the hardest clue yet . . . and it's almost dark!"

" 'Flora, fauna, fin, and feather'?" read Russell. "What are they?"

Meg chewed on the end of her pencil and studied her notebook.

WHAT DO YOU THINK THE LAST CLUE MEANS?

"It's about the first four clues," began Meg. "Flora is plants, that must be the poison ivy clue. Fauna is wildlife, that's the fox clue."

"I get it!" cried Russell. "Fin is the fish clue."

"And feather is the arrow clue," added Tina. "*So?*"

"So we have to put all the clues together," explained Meg. "I'm not sure how, but I've got them all here in my knapsack." She reached in and pulled out the four clues.

"I still don't get it," Tina sighed, as they gazed at the clues. "What's there to put together?"

DO YOU HAVE ANY IDEAS?

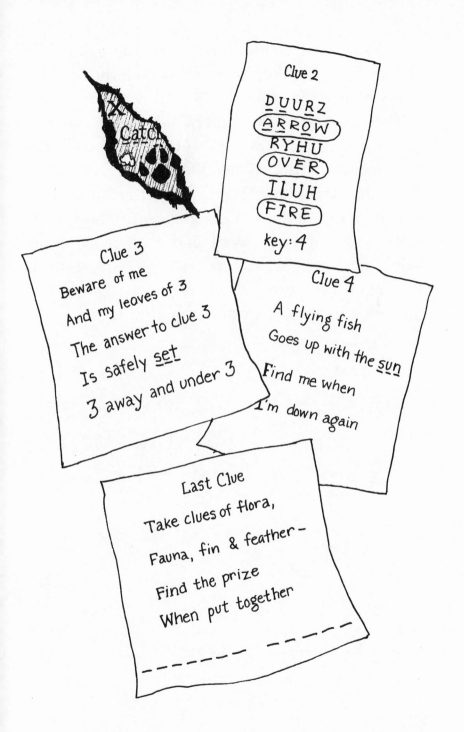

Clue 2

D U U R Z
(A R R O W)
R Y H U
(O V E R)
I L U H
(F I R E)

key: 4

Clue 3
Beware of me
And my leaves of 3
The answer to clue 3
Is safely set
3 away and under 3

Clue 4
A flying fish
Goes up with the sun
Find me when
I'm down again

Last Clue
Take clues of flora,
Fauna, fin & feather —
Find the prize
When put together

_ _ _ _ _ _ _ _ _

X Catc...

"Look!" Meg pointed at each of the clues. "On every clue there are three letters underlined. I bet that's what you're supposed to put together."

They all studied the underlined words.

"A cat with an arrow at sunset?" Russell said a few minutes later. "Ridiculous! We'd never find that."

"Wait," said Meg. "Maybe the letters fit in these spaces at the bottom of the last clue. They would make a seven-letter word and then a five-letter word." She got out three pencils and her notebook, then ripped out three sheets of paper. "Quick, let's try to figure out what words would fit in here."

cat aro
act tac
nat rat
rest rate
rot art
state suns
cart · case
oar crust
crane seat
5 letters!
7 letters!
star set?

CAT AROSUNSET
AROCATSETSUN
SUNAROSETCAN
STONE TENTS
RACES TRACE
ROTTEN SCARE
CRANE NOSES
RESTORANT
CRATERS RATS
TEASERS

They all scribbled furiously.

Do-do-dodedo-do-do-dodedo!

"The bugle call for meeting down at the campfire!" Tina exclaimed.

"More camp songs when we have a mystery to solve," moaned Russell.

Meg kept scribbling in her notebook. Suddenly she sat up straight. "I think I know where the prize is hidden."

WHERE?

catarosunset

12 letters to unscramble
to make two words

_ _ _ _ _ _ _   _ _ _ _ _

scatter   sunae
contest   arasu
outcast   snear
cartons   stuea
casters   taron
tasters   canou
statues   acorn

"Look!" She pointed at her paper. "See what it spells when you unjumble the letters!"

"Stuart! He's the ghost!" exclaimed Russell.

"But the canoe is in the haunted old shack," Tina protested. "We can't go in there!"

"Come on," insisted Meg. "We have to find out."

Meg, Russell, and Tina headed directly for the haunted shack. By the time they arrived, it was almost dark. A full moon lit the lake and the beach was very quiet except for waves gently slapping the dock. Meg flicked on her flashlight as they slowly pushed open the door.

Meg scanned the shack with her flashlight. The canoes stacked on the floor were all too new to be Stuart's. But there was one old one sitting up in the rafters. "Perfect," thought Meg.

They pulled a small stepladder over and Meg climbed carefully up. Russell and Tina tried to hold the ladder steady, but it still wobbled. Meg slowly swept her flashlight over the inside of the canoe, until her light shone down upon a brown paper en-

velope. She reached in to grab it . . . when suddenly a loud fluttering and a terrifying screech filled the rafters!

"*Ghosts!*" screamed Tina and Russell, letting go of the ladder and flying out the door.

Meg half tumbled, half slipped down the ladder and raced out after them.

WHAT DO YOU THINK MADE THE NOISE?

"Wait!" Meg called out to Tina and Russell.

They stopped running and looked back at her. She was clutching the brown envelope in one hand, and she was in fits of laughter.

"It's not funny!" Russell looked angry as Meg caught up to them. "That place is haunted!"

"It's not!" Meg tried to stop laughing. "I'm sorry, but we all looked so funny. It's only a bunch of owls up there, a nest of baby owls!"

"Baby owls?" Tina echoed in disbelief.

"Yep . . . up in the rafters. *That's* who's haunting the canoe shack. And look, I've got the prize!" She held up the envelope. "I wonder what it is."

They all stared with curiosity at the envelope.

"Let's open it with everybody else," suggested Russell.

Meg and Tina quickly agreed, and the three friends set off for the campfire.

"We found the prize!" declared Meg as they walked up to the circle of campers gathered around the fire.

"What, how could you?"

"But you burned the clue!"

"How could you solve it?"

Everybody asked questions all at once.

"I thought you three were sick all day." Tim looked puzzled.

"They *were*," said Ms. Kane.

"I'm sorry I ruined the clues," Meg apologized to everyone. She proudly handed Tim the envelope. "Here's the prize."

No one said a word as Tim opened up the envelope and pulled out the prize. "Tickets to the State Fair!" he shouted and held them up for everybody to see. "And the Fourth of July fireworks start in one hour! We'd better hurry. How about a round of applause for our three detectives!"

"YEAH!"

"Okay, everybody," announced Tim. "Grab your Camp Crescent sweatshirts and get on the bus. You too, Ms. Kane. Let's GO!"

On the bus, everybody crowded around Meg, Russell, and Tina to hear how they figured out the treasure hunt. When they had finished explaining the clues, the whole busload began singing the new camp song.

> What Camp do we love the most?
> Camp Creepy, Camp Creepy!
> Swimming, hiking, and a ghost!
> Camp Creepy, Camp Creepy!

"I bet we'll be the only camp in the state with a real ghost!" someone in the back shouted.

"Meg," whispered Russell. "We forgot to tell them about the baby owls."

The three friends thought about it for a second.

"Nah . . . that'll be our secret!"

TINA, RUSSELL AND ME
CAMP CREEPY-FIRST SUMMER

July 15

Dear Mom and Dad,
     Sorry I've been too busy
to write. I have a lot of friends
here and we do a lot of neat
things. We even solved a
mystery and found tickets
to the State Fair to see a giant
fireworks display. It was great.
We're all going to write each other
and come back next summer.
Give Skip a big hug--hi Peter
          Gotta fly-- bye xoxo
                  Meg

Meg Mackintosh
    Chipmunks
Camp Crescent Creepy
Belden, Maine
04856

Mr. + Mrs. J. Mackintosh
      P.O. Box 222
Foster, Rhode Island
          02825
POST CARD

60